They're Dropping Bombs Not Ham Sandwiches

A Two Act Play By Michael Nash

Červená Barva Press
P.O. Box 440357
W. Somerville, MA 02144-3222

www.cervenabarvapress.com

Bookstore: www.thelostbookshelf.com

Cover Design: William J. Kelle

Production Interns: Jackie Hall and Caitlin Jackson

ISBN: 978-0-578-00416-7

Library of Congress Control Number: 2009930825

Bridge is reprinted by permission and has been published
in the chapbook, *Oh Angel* (U Šoku Štampa, 2005), and in
the literary journal *Blackbox*.

They're Dropping Bombs Not Ham Sandwiches

A TWO ACT PLAY BY MICHAEL NASH

This play is dedicated to my good friend Gloria Mindock, who has written a poem, *Bridge*, which concludes the first act. Many thanks!

A heart-rending awareness of World War Two as seen through the eyes of an elderly hospital patient. His recollections are shared with a youth who is, as the play, which is set in 1989, eventually reveals, a victim of a terrorist bomb attack in Northern Ireland. Scenes from the war years are illustrated by poetry, dialogue and action, in fantasy sequences, enacted by the two central characters and three of the hospital staff. An oft-times funny, poignant and thought-provoking play.

The play is set in the corridor of a hospital. Two chairs SL are the only items of furniture. A notice board adorns the wall SC. Part of the wall from SC to SR slides open to reveal a separate performance area beyond. There are two exits each side of the stage and these can be found DSR, CSR, DSL, CSL.

CAST

MIKE	An elderly war veteran
ROB	A youth in his late teens
NURSE	In her early twenties
SISTER	In her early thirties
DOCTOR	In his early forties

ACT ONE

DOCTOR:

Watch him closely. He'll probably be all right but we must be prepared for the worst. Today, as, no doubt, you are aware, is the anniversary of when it happened....

SISTER:

Yes, doctor....

DOCTOR:

We must be vigilant....

SISTER:

I have assigned a nurse to keep observation. She's familiar with the case and is....

DOCTOR:

Fully capable of coping in an emergency?

SISTER:

Yes, doctor.

DOCTOR:

Good. This could be the turning point....

BOY:

Down the corridor and turn right. All very well but which corridor? Worse than a bloody rabbit warren this place. Never have liked hospitals. Never been in one. Not until....

SISTER:

I understand.

BOY:

No. Never. Nurse! Huh. Did you see that? Her rushing past. Hardly time to stop. No time to waste answering questions from a chap like me.....

MAN:
Always busy in here....

BOY:
Only one thing for it. Ferret around a bit. I've got time. Visiting's not for some half an hour or so. Typical of the buses. I thought I'd catch an early one. Didn't want to be late. So the bus ran on time. Half an hour! So. I'm bound to find my bearings by then. Christ! Don't go much on that smell. Gets up your nose. I wouldn't want to spend longer than necessary in here....

MAN:
You soon get use to it....

BOY:
Excuse me nurse. Nurse! She's gone. No time to waste answering....

MAN:
It's always busy in here....

BOY:
Answering questions from chaps like me.   Did you say something?

MAN:
It's always busy in here.

BOY:
Oh...

MAN:
Especially today. They're expecting some sort of crisis. I overheard a doctor speaking to one of the sisters....

BOY:
More bomb threats?

MAN:

Something like that. Casualty's just along there. And they got a special treatment centre for burns and....

BOY:

You a patient?

MAN:

What? No.

BOY:

You seem to know a lot about the place....

MAN:

Yes. My wife's been in here a few weeks now. I come in every day to visit....

BOY:

Where's Anderson Ward?

MAN:

She's in Nightingale Ward.

BOY:

I've come in to see my brother.

MAN:

Next to Anderson. Down the corridor and turn right.

BOY:

Oh. That's what the nurse said. Come to see your wife, have you? Anything serious?

MAN:

Cancer.

BOY:

My brother got shot up over in Belfast. Just been transferred to this place. They reckoned it would be better if he were nearer home. Cancer, you say. Sorry to hear it. Do you smoke?

MAN:

No.

BOY:

Go on. Have one!

MAN:

Your brother's in the army, then?

BOY:

Yes. But I don't think he'll stay in. Not after what happened over there.

MAN:

I was in the army. During the war....

BOY:

Oh.

MAN:

Had to do my bit for King and....

BOY:

From what you see in the films those were the days, eh?

MAN:

She was a real picture....

BOY:

Wouldn't care to have to stay here. That smell....

MAN:

Better than being on the streets....safer.

BOY:

It's not safe anywhere....

MAN:

A real beauty....

BOY:

Never know when they're going to strike next. If only I....

MAN:

And now....

SISTER:

Keep an eye on him, nurse, but don't make it too obvious to him that he is being observed. Report any changes in his behaviour directly to me....

NURSE:

Yes sister. Certainly....

BOY:

Sure you don't want a fag?

MAN:

No!

BOY:

I'm going to have one....

MAN:

You can't....

BOY:

Who says? It's my life....

MAN:

This is a hospital....

BOY:

Tell me something new....

MAN:

So you can't smoke in here!

BOY:

Bet most of the nurses and that do....

MAN:

Not in the corridor....

BOY:

I'll go outside then....

MAN:

I used to but....

BOY:

9

Which is the way out?

MAN:

I haven't since they discovered my Barbara....

BOY:

Do you think there'll be a new spate of bombing?

MAN:

Dunno. It's safe in here, though....

BOY:

It's not safe anywhere.

MAN:

Bombs were dropping everywhere....

BOY:

I don't like the idea of more bombing....

MAN:

During the war....

BOY:

Not after what's happened...

MAN:

I was in the army....

BOY:

It terrifies me. Just the thought of it. No sod's safe on the streets nowadays....

MAN:

It's safe in here....

BOY:

I bet the war years were good years....

MAN:

I wouldn't say that....

BOY:

But I've seen all the films....

MAN:

Films! Hollywood gloss. How John Wayne won the war single-handed! It wasn't all heroes and the like. I know. I could tell you a few stories of what it was really like....

BOY:

Why don't you? We've got plenty of time. I'd like to hear some of your views. I mean. We see so much of it on the telly. But that's all, well, fantasy, I suppose? Not like getting it first hand from someone who was actually there. It's like my brother. He tells me things about Northern Ireland the papers would never dare to print.

MAN:

Or the Government wanted to keep quiet about....

BOY:

His CO led the platoon straight into an ambush knowing full well what was to happen. Even said that he expected it. Marched them in like lambs to the slaughter. He could have avoided it! He could have surprised the enemy. Stupid bastard! It's his fault that my brother is in here now. Robin's always talking about it. Over and over again. I've heard it so many times. Makes me feel as though I were there myself....

MAN:

It's safe in here....

SISTER:

The Second World War was the most terrifying reality of modern times. It was the first global conflict to be fought with equal intensity in all parts of the world and it affected the lives of everyone on earth....

DOCTOR:

Peace in our time.

NURSE:

Thank God.

BOY:

So what happened after that geezer...?

MAN:

Chamberlain....

BOY:

That's right. Well, what happened when he returned from Munich holding that famous piece of paper with Hitler's signature on it? What did they reckon would happen? What did you think?

MAN:
Well, I knew trouble was brewing. After all, the papers were full of it. But the Government knew different....

BOY:
They always do....

MAN:
Mind you, old Adolf was pushing his luck a bit far to my way of thinking. World supremacy! The master race! We didn't want that. After all, we were British! We've never been a nation wanting world domination....

BOY:
What about the people?

MAN:
A great Empire!

BOY:
What did they think?

MAN:
Generally, I suppose, the people, as a nation, were oblivious to any possibility that we would be at war within a year....

NURSE:
Today was a beautiful day.

SISTER:
The sky was a brilliant blue for the first time for weeks and weeks.

NURSE:
Posters flapping on the railings tell the world that Hitler speaks.

SISTER:
And we cannot take it in.

NURSE:
We go to our daily jobs to the dull refrain of the caption....

DOCTOR:

War!

NURSE:

Buzzing around us as from hidden insects and we think....

SISTER:

This must be wrong. It has happened before.

NURSE:

And just like before we must be dreaming. It was long ago these flies buzzed like this....

SISTER:

So why are they still bombarding the ears if not the eyes?

DOCTOR:

And we laugh it off and go round town in the evening and this we say is on me. Something out of the usual? A Pimm's Number One? A Picon?

BOY:

But did you see the latest?

DOCTOR:

You mean whether Cobb has just bust the record or do you mean that the Australians have lost their last by ten wickets....

SISTER:

Or do you mean that the Autumn fashions....?

BOY:

No. We don't mean anything like that again. No. What we mean is Hodza, Heinlein, Hitler, the Maginot Line, the heavy panic that cramps the lungs and presses the collar down the spine.

NURSE:

And when we go out into Piccadilly Circus they are selling and buying the late special editions snatched and read abruptly beneath the electric signs as crude as fate.

DOCTOR:

And the individual, powerless, has to exert the powers of will and choice and choose between enormous evils, either of which depends upon somebody else's voice.

SISTER:

The cylinders are racing in the presses.

BOY:

The mines are laid.

DOCTOR:

The ribbon plumbs the fallen fathoms of Wall Street.

NURSE & SISTER:

And you and I are afraid.

MAN:

Course, I wasn't afraid. I put my trust in old Neville Chamberlain. He knew what he was up to all right. Just needed the right chance. And, as far as we were concerned Hitler was all for peace. Least, that's what he said. And most of us believed it. Our Elsie did, anyhow. That's my sister. I remember a few months before war broke out she had been on holiday in Switzerland....

BOY:

I went there with my school. Interlaken....

MAN:

Lucerne....

BOY:

No! It was Interlaken! At Easter....

MAN:

Elsie went to Lucerne....

BOY:

Right....

MAN:

Met up with this German fellow. Student of some sort. All very romantic from what she said. They bumped into each other on some kind of covered bridge. She sent me a postcard of it. Got it in my pocket somewhere. I always carry it around with me. See. All the paintings hanging from the rafters. She was trying to take a photograph, stepped back and there he was. Love at first sight. I remember her coming home filled with stories of how she was going

14

to marry him and go and live in Germany. How she'd have a better life. Nothing came of it. The war saw to that.   Never heard no more about him.

BOY:
Think we went there. Sure we did?

MAN:
Got himself killed, I suppose? Elsie married a Yank instead.   Not seen either of them since forty-five. She went back with him. Living in Chicago. I do get a card every Christmas....

NURSE:
On the evening of the second of September Chamberlain addressed the House of Commons. MP's expected to hear that war had been declared. Instead, it was announced that if the German government would agree to withdraw their troops from Poland the British government would forget everything that had happened and diplomacy could start again. Chamberlain sat down in silence.

DOCTOR:
Greenwood, rising to speak for Labour, was greeted with a shout from Amery.

MAN:
Speak for England, Arthur!

NURSE:
Afterwards Greenwood warned Chamberlain that there would be no holding the House if war were not declared. The Cabinet met late at night and resolved that an ultimatum should be sent to Germany....

BOY:
That's nice.

MAN:
What?

BOY:
Getting a card from your sister.

MAN:
Every Christmas without fail.

BOY:

Nice.

MAN:

But....

BOY:

Be nice to see her after all this time....

MAN:

She's given up writing on them. Their names, now, are always printed on in black....

DOCTOR:

The British ultimatum was delivered in Berlin at 9am on the third of September....

BOY:

What does it matter?

MAN:

But....

BOY:

As long as you receive them each year it shows you're not forgotten.

MAN:

I wrote to her a few months ago but never got an answer....

NURSE:

The German government made no reply, and the ultimatum expired at 11am.

MAN:

I remember listening to old Neville on the wireless. He said the reason for war was....

DOCTOR:

A situation in which no word by Germany's ruler can be trusted and no people or country can feel itself safe has become intolerable.

BOY:

I thought there was supposed to be peace in our time? We don't want war! Surely there's been too much bloody bombing?

NURSE:

The French trailed their ally and declared war at 5pm....

MAN:

She did well to marry that Yank. Nice fellow. Looked smart in his uniform. No doubt why she took to him....

BOY:

All the women seem to go for a uniform!

MAN:

Alex. Alex Dawson. Quite a charmer. Can't help wondering what happened to the Jerry bloke though? Suppose he returned to the Fatherland to do his bit? We all had our duty to do....

BOY:

To fight for one's country....

MAN:

Regardless of which side we were on....

BOY:

To fight in order to secure a lasting peace....

NURSE:

It will be alright. Just wait and see. No harm can come to you now....

MAN:

God willing....

NURSE:

Don't worry. I'm here to take care of you....

MAN:

Elsie did tell me his name. What was it?

BOY:

My brother can tell you things you're never likely to read in the papers....

MAN:
Was it Karl? Something like that. What does it matter? When you reach my age you want to forget. Huh! How can we forget? Easy to remember what happened then. Have difficulty, though, in remembering what happened yesterday! Part of growing old. Living in the past. Only the young have a future....

BOY:
I have no future.....

DOCTOR:
It has begun....

NURSE:
I never thought it would happen....

SISTER:
We must be prepared for the worst....

NURSE:
I'll keep watch....

SISTER:
I want to know immediately if there is any change....

NURSE:
I understand....

SISTER:
We can't be too careful. Any sudden attack and....

NURSE:
Surely it won't last?

SISTER:
Only time will tell....

MAN:
Anyway, I'll call him Karl. Not that his real name matters. He went back to his homeland and Elsie heard nothing more about him. I've often wondered what would have happened to her if she'd married him? She'd have been well and truly caught up in the thick of it....

BOY:

Eh?

MAN:

Interned in some camp for the duration, I suppose?

BOY:

I hate people staring at me....

MAN:

What?

BOY:

That nurse....

MAN:

I thought you wanted to hear about my wartime experiences?

BOY:

I do.

MAN:

Then why aren't you listening?

BOY:

She seems to be watching every move we make? It's okay to wait here, isn't it? We're not in the way or anything?

MAN:

I always sit here.

BOY:

I could do with a cuppa.

MAN:

They sometimes bring me a cup of tea.

BOY:

The smell in here makes you feel dry....

MAN:

You'll get used to it....

BOY:

Nurse!

MAN:

In time....

BOY:

Nurse!

MAN:

When you've been here as long as....

NURSE:

Did you want something?

MAN:

I....

BOY:

I could do with a drink. I'm parched. Not used to....

NURSE:

I'll see what I can do....

BOY:

I'm waiting to see my brother....

NURSE:

I see....

BOY:

He's in Anderson Ward....

MAN:

Remember the Anderson shelters?

BOY:

When can I see him? I've been waiting a very long time and....

NURSE:

I'll get you some tea. Or would you prefer coffee?

BOY:

A choice?

MAN:

You always get a choice in here.

BOY:

I'll have tea....

MAN:

May I have some as well, please?

NURSE:

Of course. Stay here....

BOY:

And, then, can I see my brother?

NURSE:

Soon. You must be patient....

BOY:

She seems nice. Quite friendly.

MAN:

Yes....

BOY:

Wonder if she's got a boyfriend? I wouldn't mind....

MAN:

Are you more interested in that nurse than in hearing my story? I can always move to another place....

BOY:

Nice legs. Perhaps she fancies me? That's why she kept staring!

MAN:

I'm going....

BOY:

No! Don't do that. I'm sorry. Please go on. Did you volunteer when war broke out?

MAN:

No. Conscription was introduced a few months before the outbreak. Part of the preparation in case of hostilities. Must have been round about Easter? I was working for a builder then. Just starting an apprenticeship....

BOY:

You were called up at the beginning then?

MAN:

Should have been a farmer or a miner. Wouldn't be where I am today if I had....

BOY:

Well? Were you?

MAN:

What?

BOY:

Called up?

MAN:

Not at first. Not until the October. Just after my eighteenth birthday when the buff envelope from the Ministry of Defence arrived. I was to go into the Royal Artillery. Didn't get any choice. Straight into where they put you. A lot of us there were. Still wet behind the ears. Thrown together and whipped up, in no time at all, to form a fighting force. Hardly had time to know what had hit us! A bit of basic training and, then, Bob's your uncle, we're shipped off to France with only a rousing speech to send us on our way....

BOY:

Where's she got with that cup of tea?

MAN:

A rousing speech. Every man had to do his duty! Take up your guns men of courage and might! Face the enemy! Fight! Fight! Fight! Be not afraid of death! God is on our side! Huh. All right for those left behind. What did they know of the bullets and the uncertainty?

BOY:

I'm going to look for her.

MAN:

What?

BOY:

I want my drink....

MAN:

Don't go. She'll bring it when she gets a moment. They get very busy. Can't expect them to bother too much with us. They have their patients to think about first. Sit down. I'll tell you more.

BOY:

Okay. But I really could do with a drink of something. My throat's bloody dry! It's got to be the smell. Wouldn't fancy having to stay here. I bet my brother hates it. Did I tell you his name? Robin....

MAN:

Nice name. Sort of name I'd give to a son. I'd like to meet him and have a chat....

BOY:

You can't! He's not allowed visitors....

DOCTOR:

How's the new patient settling in, sister? Any problems?

SISTER:

No. He appears quiet enough....

DOCTOR:

That's good. Incidentally, sister, I was wondering if you'd care to go for a drink tonight?

SISTER:

I'd love to....

DOCTOR:

I'll call for you at eight....

SISTER:

Nurse! Where are you taking those?

NURSE:

To them. They asked for some tea....

SISTER:

Only for the boy. Don't want to encourage....

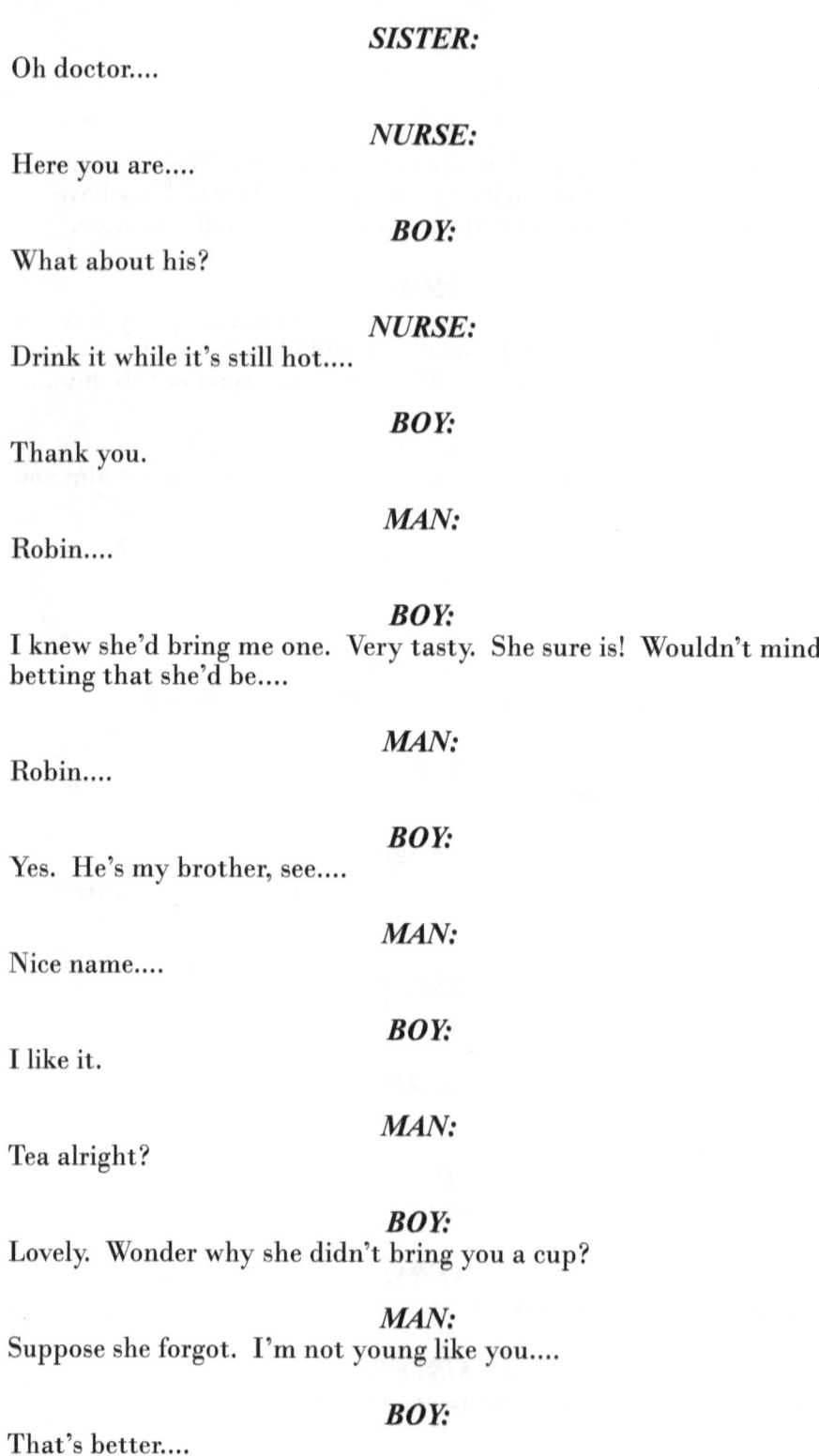

SISTER:

Oh doctor....

NURSE:

Here you are....

BOY:

What about his?

NURSE:

Drink it while it's still hot....

BOY:

Thank you.

MAN:

Robin....

BOY:

I knew she'd bring me one. Very tasty. She sure is! Wouldn't mind betting that she'd be....

MAN:

Robin....

BOY:

Yes. He's my brother, see....

MAN:

Nice name....

BOY:

I like it.

MAN:

Tea alright?

BOY:

Lovely. Wonder why she didn't bring you a cup?

MAN:

Suppose she forgot. I'm not young like you....

BOY:

That's better....

MAN:

Too old to be worth the trouble. Don't matter that I did my bit.

BOY:

Were you excited by the prospect of going to war? Quite an adventure I suppose? Better that the mundane routine of basic training?

MAN:

Mundane?

BOY:

Yes. Well Robin reckons it was. He's my brother....

MAN:

You told me his name....

BOY:

Oh yes. Just testing! Seeing that you're paying attention! He reckons, anyhow, that the only time he has fun is when he's doing a spell of active duty.

MAN:

Fun?

BOY:

Some bloody fun!

MAN:

Look what's happened to him....

BOY:

Bloody bastards! I'd like to get my hands on them! I'd show them what for....

MAN:

The only good thing about basic training was at least I got the chance of seeing my Barbara most weekends. We'd met a few weeks before the war started. Did I tell you? I fell in love with her the moment I first saw her....

BOY:

That was nice. I had a girl once....

MAN:

She was a nurse. I'd been taken to outpatients after falling from a ladder at the site. The gaffer thought I'd busted my arm. I was taken to the hospital and there she was. I wish she were still....

BOY:

This hospital?

MAN:

What?

BOY:

Was this the hospital?

MAN:

No. We were living in Southampton. That's where I was born. Moved up to London during the war....

BOY:

Thought you said you were shipped off to France?

MAN:

Barbara and I got wed just after Dunkirk and she came up here to help with the injured. I was one of the lucky ones who got evacuated. Few scratches but nothing serious. Had some leave during which time we moved into a small flat near....

BOY:

Oh.

MAN:

Anyhow. I'm jumping the gun a bit. I was telling you about basic training, wasn't I?

BOY:

That's right....

MAN:

We were kept on our toes day and night. I can still hear that sergeant shouting his orders at us. Will I ever forget?

DOCTOR:

Take your guns, stand in line!

MAN/BOY:

Marching on the spot is fine!

DOCTOR:

Shoulders back, chests well out!

MAN/BOY:

Altogether, now, let's shout! Naming of parts! Naming of parts! today we have naming of parts! And we're going to fight the enemy, we're going to fight the foe!

FEMALES:

Such wonderful, brave young men we see!

MAN/BOY:

But we don't want to go!

DOCTOR:

No talking in the ranks! Did you hear me? This ain't no Sunday School parade! This is the safety-catch, released with a flick of the thumb! Fingers are forbidden!

MAN/BOY:

So stick them up your....

DOCTOR:

No talking in the ranks! Naming of parts! Naming of parts! Today we have naming of parts!

MAN/BOY:

And we're going to fight the enemy!

FEMALES:

You're going to fight the foe!

MAN/BOY:

Such wonderful, brave young men are we!

FEMALES:

But you don't want to go!

MAN/BOY:

Fingers up! Fingers down!

DOCTOR:

Private Green and Private Brown! Stand in line, chests well out!

MAN/BOY:

Altogether, now, let's shout! The safety-catch! The safety-catch! Flick of the thumb! The safety-catch!

ALL:

Naming of parts! Naming of parts! Today we have naming of parts!

DOCTOR:

And this is called the bolt! It opens the breech this thing! We slide it to and fro and call it easing the spring!

ALL:

And we're going to fight the enemy, we're going to fight the foe!

DOCTOR:

Left! Right! Left! Right! Quick march!

MAN:

He sure put us through our paces. Not a bad sort of bloke really. He made us train hard but, I reckon, we were better men for it. I can tell you this much. Not one of us were afraid to face Jerry. We were quite capable of giving him as good as he gave us and that's a fact!

BOY:

What happened to you after Dunkirk?

MAN:

Spent a couple of weeks in hospital. Nothing serious. Shock, they said. Wed Barbara on June the thirtieth and then, before I knew it, I was posted to an artillery unit near Dover....

NURSE:

Dunkirk was a great deliverance....

MAN:

And it great disaster!

DOCTOR:

In the midst of our defeat glory came to our Island people, united and unconquerable. There was a white glow, overpowering, sublime, which ran through our Island from end to end. And the tale of Dunkirk will shine in whatever records are preserved of our affairs.

MAN:

Dunkirk was a defeat!

SISTER:

Which completed a German campaign that had captured one million prisoners....

MAN:

And, then, about six weeks after my posting, all hell broke loose. Hitler was determined to conquer us. Operation Sealion. His invasion plan. Goring was sure his Luftwaffe pilots could set the way. Mind you, they had the RAF to contend with. Bloody good fighting force. I wouldn't have minded joining them.
Nearest I got, though, was on the anti-aircraft guns down in Dover. Suppose you could say....

BOY:

Wonder what it would have been like?

MAN:

What?

BOY:

If the Germans had overrun this country....

MAN:

Doesn't bear thinking about....

BOY:

They've done alright for themselves. We'd probably have been better off....

MAN:

You're talking rubbish. The Nazis were....

BOY:

Wouldn't have all these foreigners....

MAN:

Nothing wrong with them....

BOY:

Be easier to get a job....

NURSE:

I'll take your cup if you've finished with it?

BOY:

Nice tea, thanks....

MAN:

They did well for us. We had a couple of darkies down with us in Dover. I got on all right with them. Don't know what all the fuss is about. Barbara had some of the women working with her. She said, many times, that they made the best nurses. Where are you off to?

BOY:

Thought I'd take a look down the corridor to see if it's visiting yet....

MAN:

They'll let you know. A nurse'll come round with a bell. No. She rings the bell at the end of visiting....

BOY:

Go on with your story then. I promise I won't go away.

MAN:

They don't like people wandering around....

BOY:

Why?

MAN:

I guess we did our best to help the boys flying above....

DOCTOR:

This is a damned inhuman sort of war! I've been fighting in a dressing gown most of the night. I cannot see the guns. I cannot see the guns! I've been watching for a symbol thrown upon a screen. I cannot see the planes. I cannot see the planes! I've been sweating in this basement room most of the night. I cannot see the guns. I cannot see the guns! I've been sifting through the facts making calculations. I cannot see the planes. I cannot see the planes! We chant our ritual words. Give orders to the guns.

SISTER:

One!

DOCTOR:

Fire!

SISTER:

Two!

DOCTOR:

Fire!

MAN:

Guns roar!

BOY:

Shells pour!

SISTER:

Three!

DOCTOR:

Fire!

SISTER:

Four!

DOCTOR:

Fire!

MAN:

Planes roar.

BOY:

Bombs pour!

SISTER:

Ghosts answer. The guns roar abruptly. And an aircraft waging war inhumanely from nearly five miles height meets our bouquet of death.

BOY:

Oh, my God! I don't want to die!

MAN:

We have no choice!

NURSE:

Doctor! Sister! A new spate of bomb attacks is expected!

BOY:

The bastards! We've got to stop the bastards!

DOCTOR:

I've been fighting in a dressing-gown most of the night. I cannot see the planes....

NURSE:

Earth opens where the squandered bombs fall wide and all our view's a burning mass. Each fairy-lamp incendiary that falls glitters every colour like celebration fireworks. Only the sudden metal weight of fear brings us back to reality, keeping us awake as we sit staring out with hearts pounding....

BOY:

What's it all about? Where will it end?

DOCTOR:

Fire!

BOY:

I don't want....

MAN:

Calm down.

BOY:

I'm sorry. I hope I didn't alarm you? It's just that you make everything seem so real and I can't help thinking about my brother. He got shot up you now....

MAN:

Don't worry....

BOY:

We're very close....

MAN:

You'll be seeing him soon. Just a matter of being patient....

BOY:

I don't like the smell of this place. I need to get out for some fresh air....

MAN:

You can't do that!

BOY:

Who says?

MAN:

I haven't finished.

BOY:

Who says?

MAN:

Teamwork....

BOY:

What?

MAN:

The Battle of Britain. Teamwork. We all did our bit to secure a victory. Servicemen and civilians alike. We all pulled together. Didn't want the Nazis goose-stepping their way through London....

BOY:

Probably be better off! I nearly joined the National Front before....

MAN:

It was bad enough having them in the Channel Islands, on the doorstep as it were....

BOY:

An uncle of mine comes from Jersey. He was there for some of the Occupation. Says the Germans weren't too bad....

MAN:

A collaborator?

BOY:

No! In fact he managed to escape to the mainland with the help of a German soldier he befriended. The Jerry was as much against Hitler as....

MAN:

There were a lot like him....

BOY:

So Uncle Ted joined the Royal Navy. He was a fisherman before the war so he was quite used to the sea.

MAN:

Our Elsie said they were alright....

BOY:

Afterwards, he returned to the island and opened up a bar in St. Helier with that same German. He died, though, before I was born. I've been over there. Just before I was....

MAN:

Wonder what happened to that chap she met in Lucerne?

BOY:

Before my brother was posted to Northern Ireland....

DOCTOR:

When the bloom is off the garden, and I'm fighting in the sky, when the lawns and flower beds harden, and when weak birds starve and die, and death-roll will grow longer, eyes will be moist and red. And the more I kill, the longer I shall miss my friends who are dead.

MAN:

Clearing - Black Section Patrol - Bass Rock!

BOY:

Leaps heart! After shock run stumbling. Snatch your helmet. Run smoothly to the grumbling of a dozen Merlin charged air. You are there by 'Z'. Down hard on the behind your oxygen snout. Click, click, click. You feel the harness is fixed. Round the wing and....

DOCTOR:

Out of the cockpit you!

BOY:
Clamber the rung and the wing as if a wasp has stung you. Hop and jump into the cockpit. Split second to spike the Sutton harness holes. One. Two. Three. Four. Thrust with your hand to the throttle open....

DOCTOR:
Operations called and spoken....

BOY:
Nurse!

MAN:
I remember watching the planes as they fought overhead....

BOY:
Nurse!

MAN:
A beautiful sight! Like birds. Graceful. Jerry chasing one of our boys....

BOY:
Nurse!

MAN:
One of our lads chasing Jerry....

BOY:
Just then I saw the bloody Hun.

NURSE:
You saw the Hun? You, light and easy, carving the soundless daylight?

BOY:
I was breezy when I saw that Hun.

NURSE:
Oh wonder pattern of stress, of nerve poise, flyer overtaking time.

BOY:
He came out under nine-tenths cloud, but I was higher.

NURSE:

Did Michelangelo aspire, painting the laughing cumulus, to ride the majesty of air?

BOY:

He was a trier I'll give him that, the Hun.

DOCTOR:

So, you convert ultimate sky to air speed, drift and cover.

BOY:

Sure!

NURSE:

With tricky tools of God and lover.

BOY:

I let him have a sharp, four-second burst, closing to fifty yards. He went on fire.

NURSE:

Your deadly petals painted, you exert a simple stature.

DOCTOR:

Man high, without pride, you pick your way through heaven and the dirt.

MAN:

He burnt out in the air. That's how the poor sod died....

BOY:

Nurse! Nurse!

NURSE:

Not long now....

BOY:

I'm tired of waiting. I have to....

NURSE:

Not long now....

BOY:

I want to see my brother. I have to take care of him. He needs me. I feel responsible....

MAN:

Like birds....

BOY:

Very nice....

MAN:

The Battle of Britain they called it....

BOY:

Wonder what time she gets off duty?

MAN:

Fought and won....

BOY:

Reckon she fancies me. Could be the beginning of something good.

MAN:

But it was not the beginning of the end of the war, it was the end of the beginning....

DOCTOR:

Never in the field of human conflict was so much owed by so many to so few....

NURSE:

Do not despair for Johnny-head-in-air. He sleeps as sound as Johnny-underground. Fetch out no shroud for Johnny-in-the-cloud. And keep your tears for him in after years. Better, by far, for Johnny-the-bright-star, to keep your head, and see his children fed.

SISTER:

Less said the better. The bill unpaid, the dead letter. No roses at the end for Smith, my friend. Last words don't matter, and there are none to flatter. Words will not fill the post of Smith the ghost. For Smith, our brother, only son of loving mother, the ocean lifted, stirred, leaving no word.

BOY:

Nurse!

MAN:

What now?

BOY:

I want to....

MAN:

All in good time. All in good time.

BOY:

Nurse!

NURSE:

What is it?

BOY:

When can I see him?

NURSE:

The doctor's on his rounds now....

BOY:

Sod the doctor!

NURSE:

Be patient....

BOY:

Stay and talk to me....

NURSE:

I can't. I must work. You're alright with Mr. Wallace....

BOY:

But?

NURSE:

I must work....

BOY:

I think I'm going off her. She's got no time for the likes of me....

MAN:

Less said the better....

BOY:

Sod off!

MAN:

The Battle of Britain over and I was able to spend my birthday on leave up in London with my Barbara....

BOY:

I still fancy her though....

MAN:

She was a smashing girl....

BOY:

Bet she could teach me a thing or two? Or I her?

MAN:

We had a nice little flat near Paddington Station....

BOY:

I bet the doctor's had his....

MAN:

She made it really lovely....

BOY:

Nice apartment. Soft music. Wine. Flowers....

MAN:

Pink roses on the wallpaper. Only two rooms. We shared the kitchen and the bathroom.

BOY:

Lucky sod!

MAN:

Elsie came to see us whenever she could. Before the Americans arrived and she got involved with Alex....

BOY:

Some blokes get all the luck....

MAN:

Barbara was a nurse....

BOY:

Not a bad life being a doctor. Surrounded by all those nurses in their starched uniforms, clean, neat, black stockings....

MAN:

My Florence Nightingale I used to call her. We were happy the two of us even though the country was at war and we only got to see each other every so often....

BOY:

Quite turns me on....

MAN:

You listening?

BOY:

Of course I am.

MAN:

Didn't think you were?

BOY:

I am! Tell me some more. I'm really interested. Honest. Anything to keep you happy. Anything to pass the time....

MAN:

Do you know, son, it's a pleasure to talk to you. I only wish I had a son like you....

BOY:

Sure....

MAN:

I bet your parents are proud of you? And your brother?

BOY:

Have you any family?

MAN:

No. Barbara was pregnant, but....

BOY:

I'd like to have a kid....

MAN:

Nothing better than having a bit of company in a place like this....

BOY:

Don't think I'll be able....

MAN:

What was I saying?

BOY:

Doubt if it's impossible....

MAN:

Going up to London. On leave....

DOCTOR:

It seems to me I spend my life in stations. Going, coming, standing, waiting. Paddington, Darlington, Shrewsbury, York. I know them all most bitterly. Dawn stations with a steel light and waxen figures. Dust, stone, and clanking sounds, hiss of weary steam. Night stations, shaded light, fading pools of colour. Shadows and the shuffling of a million feet. Khaki, blue and bulky kitbags, rifles gleaming dull. Metal sound of army boots. Smoker's coughs. Titter of harlots in their silver foxes. Cases, casks, and coffins, clanging of the trolleys. Tea urns tarnished, and the greasy white of cups. Dry buns, Woodbines, Picture Post, Penguins and the blaze of magazines. Grinding sound of trains. Rattle of the platform gates. Running feet and sudden shouts, clink of glasses from the cafe. Smell of drains, tar, fish and chips and sweaty scent, honk of taxis, and the gleam of cigarettes. Iron pillars, cupolas of glass, hands and callous face says twenty-five to nine. A cigarette, a cup of tea, a bun, and my train goes at ten.

BOY:

Unless....

MAN:

And my train goes at....

BOY:

Do you get the feeling those two are watching us?

MAN:

No.

BOY:

I suppose it's alright to wait here? We're not in the way, are we?

MAN:
No.

BOY:
Of course not! How stupid of me! Didn't that nurse bring me a cup ot tea. She would have said....

MAN:
My train goes....

BOY:
There's nothing wrong with us, is there? We're getting some mighty strange looks. I hate the feeling of being watched. Almost like expecting an ambush....

MAN:
They're too busy to bother with the likes of us....

BOY:
Tell you. I don't really know why I bothered to come in here....

MAN:
To see your brother....

BOY:
He won't recognise me. It's been a bloody long time since....

MAN:
Of course he will....

BOY:
Don't see no point. I. I....

MAN:
You feeling alright? You look pale?

BOY:
What's it to do with you? I feel sick, that's all. Must be the stink. Never mind me....

MAN:
Shall I call the nurse?

BOY:
Leave it out, will you! Get on with your bloody story!

MAN:

I....

BOY:

I bet you had some good times?

MAN:

What?

BOY:

You and your missus? Dancing and the like?

MAN:

No....

BOY:

You must have done! You're not going to tell me that you spent all your leave cooped up in two bleeding rooms?

MAN:

No. We preferred the....

BOY:

Yes?

MAN:

We preferred the theatre. Nice musical or a variety show. Took the mind away from the realities of war. It's best to forget things now and then. Memories can be so hurtful. It's best to forget! That's what I'm always being told....

BOY:

Forget? You seem to be remembering things very well....

MAN:

I remember when they brought me the news about....

BOY:

Those two are still watching.

MAN:

Bloody Germans had no thought about the civilians they were murdering. Barbara was only....

BOY:

I 'm going over and ask them what they're staring at?

MAN:

We saw some good shows. Barbara and I. We were happy then. First class entertainment. A damn sight better than the rubbish they churn out nowadays....

BOY:

Makes you feel uncomfortable....

MAN:

I took Barbara to the Palladium. That's some place! We saw Vera Lynn. Her favourite she was. Are you listening? Or am I wasting my time?

BOY:

Eh?

MAN:

Are you listening?

BOY:

Of course I am. Just don't like the way those two keep staring at us every time they pass....

MAN:

Forget it....

BOY:

They make me feel bloody uneasy.

MAN:

What's your name?

BOY:

What's it to you?

MAN:

I'd like to know, that's all. We've been chatting here for quite some time, now, and I don't even know your name.

BOY:

It's not important....

MAN:

Mine's Mike....

BOY:

If you must know it's Rob....

MAN:

Rob....

BOY:

Short for Rob - um - Robert.

MAN:

Robert.

BOY:

Do you think it's visiting yet?

MAN:

I'll go down to the ward and see what's happening....

BOY:

Don't leave me....

MAN:

I'll come back....

BOY:

I want to hear more of your story....

MAN:

I'm always in here. I'll see you again. I'll look out for you.

BOY:

Good....

MAN:

I'm always in here. I never miss a day. I never miss....

NURSE & SISTER

The angels are ripping our
bodies apart, they're butchering corpses.
Look, we can't conceal that our flesh is dying.
Insects multiply in our blood.
And if this isn't enough, We can't
talk about it.
Hands are shaky. We are afraid of
breaking down, becoming weak, and being
killed by pity.
Silence is better.
A slight wind touches us.
We can nourish ourselves with this.

There's no shame in saying nothing.
Silence is life--talk is only a wound.
No barricade here, just waiting for another part.
A different day which will happen when
we don't exist--
Please remember us tenderly...
Knock your head against a wall and
resurrect us...

END OF ACT ONE

ACT TWO

DOCTOR:
It's going to be a thick night tonight. And the night before was a thick one.

MAN:
I've just seen the padre disappearing into the 'Cock and Bull' for a quick one.

DOCTOR:
I don't mind telling you this, old boy, we got the major drinking. You probably know the amount of gin he's in the habit of sinking. And then that new MO came in, the Jewish one....

MAN:
Awful fellow!

DOCTOR:
And his wife dressed in a sort of flaming yellow. Looked a pretty warmish piece, old boy.

MAN:
No, have this one on me.

DOCTOR:
They were both so blind, and so was the major, that they could hardly see.

SISTER:
She had one of those amazing hats and a kind of silver fox fur.

BOY:
I wouldn't mind betting several fellows have had a go at her!

DOCTOR:

She made a bee-line for the major, bloody funny, old boy.

SISTER:

Asked him a lot about horses and India, you know, terribly coy.

NURSE:

And this MO fellow was mopping it up and at last he passed right out.

BOY:

Some silly old fool, behind his back, put a bottle of gin in his stout!

SISTER:

I've never seen a man go down so quick.

NURSE:

Somebody drove him home.

BOY:

His wife was almost as bad, old boy.

NURSE:

Said she felt ill and nestled up to the major.

BOY:

It's a great pity you weren't there.

SISTER:

And the padre was arguing about the order of morning and evening prayer.

BOY:

Never laughed so much in my life.

NURSE:

We went on drinking until three.

BOY:

And this woman was doing her best to sit on the major's knee!

MAN:

Let's have the blackout boards put up. And turn on the other light.

DOCTOR:

Yes I think you can count on that, old boy. Tonight'll be a thick night!

MAN:

This officer goes into see the MO....

BOY:

Excuse me, but can I have a vasectomy on the National Health?

DOCTOR:

No! We only operate on the privates!

MAN:

It was the day of the operation....

DOCTOR:

There's a risk. If anything goes wrong you could end up as a vegetable....

BOY:

Do I have a choice?

DOCTOR:

Yes. You can either be a carrot or a cabbage!

NURSE:

Our GP died last week.

SISTER:

I'm sorry to hear that.

NURSE:

It sort of destroys your confidence....

SISTER:

Why?

NURSE:

I mean, if he couldn't keep himself alive....

SISTER:

Very funny....

DOCTOR:

Long after the war we got mail from people who'd been living in occupied countries asking was it true all that laughter and gaiety coming from London during the blitz.

NURSE:

Their own propaganda was very strong and they couldn't believe it was possible.

DOCTOR:

We found we could create better propaganda simply by injecting a funny line somewhere....

NURSE:

It was far more effective than brain-washing....

DOCTOR:

Especially during the blitz....

NURSE:

Like the old gag about the two Cockneys in a top-floor apartment.

DOCTOR:

During a raid they ran downstairs to the shelter. The wife suddenly turned back....

MAN:

Where are you going?

SISTER:

I'm going back for my teeth.

MAN:

Don't be a silly old fool! They're dropping bombs not ham sandwiches!

BOY:

Well?

MAN:

Always enjoyed a good laugh....

BOY:

Did you see her?

MAN:

Who?

BOY:

Barbara.

MAN:

Got to wait....

BOY:

I can't figure out what's happening. Is this some kind of joke?
Nothing seems real....

MAN:

We've got to wait.

BOY:

It's all so bloody odd! Funny....

MAN:

We saw some good comics during the war. Me and Barbara. Went
to the Windmill. Never closed. That was the place for variety.
Always count on a good show there. Most of the older comedians
you see on television, nowadays, started at the Windmill....

BOY:

Really odd....

MAN:

And then there was the songs....

BOY:

I like a good song.

MAN:

Never lose their popularity....

BOY:

Reckon I could be a pop star....

MAN:

And didn't the people sing! It was the songs and the music - Glen
Miller he was my favourite - brought the people together. United
us. Provided us with an escape. Just like a breath of....

BOY:

Think I'll go out for a breath of fresh air....

MAN:

Took the mind far away from the realities of war. On the radio. In the papers. Nothing but war! Even at the cinema. Propaganda films. For King and Country. You couldn't get away from it....

BOY:

If only I could find my way out? This place is like a bloody rabbit warren! Can't remember how I got in here....

MAN:

Couldn't get away from it....

BOY:

They've shown all those old films on the telly. Noel Coward and the like....

MAN:

Poor Barbara and I even got news, occasionally, from Germany....

BOY:

Germany? Thought you said she'd lost touch with that Jerry bloke?

MAN:

Not him! And it was Elsie! Not Barbara!

BOY:

Sorry I spoke....

MAN:

My brother-in-law, a year or so older than me and college educated, was in the RAF. He got shot down over Holland on a bombing raid to Hamburg. Tried his best to get back to Blighty but was captured in France and sent to a POW camp in Germany....

DOCTOR:

So here I am upon the German earth beneath the German sky, and the birds flock southward, wheeling as they fly. And there are morning mists, and trees turn brown, and the winds blow and blow the dead leaves down. And lamps are earlier on and curtains drawn. And nights have frosted dew-drops on the lawn, and bonfire smoke goes crawling up on high. Just as on an English earth beneath an English sky. But here am I....

MAN:

And Arnold, that's the wife's brother, spent the duration in various camps. We got a few letters through the Red Cross....

BOY:

Always collecting they are. Standing on street corners thrusting their tins in your face....

MAN:

Mind you, he made several escape attempts. Especially when he got the news about the hospital where....

BOY:

I'd like to meet him....

MAN:

When she....

BOY:

I bet he could spin a yarn or two?

MAN:

Died.

BOY:

Oh....

MAN:

Great football fan. Killed in the Munich air disaster. Ironic really....

BOY:

Dead.

MAN:

Survived the POW camps and all that. And then killed in a plane on German soil!

BOY:

I reckon they ought to brighten this place up a bit. Bloody place feels so cold with everything painted white. Nice bit of flower-patterned wallpaper would do the trick....

MAN:

This is a hospital....

BOY:

Maybe - but why make them all like bloody morgues? I couldn't
stay here....

DOCTOR:

The pale wild roses star the banks of green and poignant poppies
startle their fields with red, while peace, like sunlight, rests on the
summer scene, though lilac, that flashed in the hedges, is dulled and
dead. In the faint sky the singing birds go over. The sheep are quiet
where the quiet grasses grow. I go to the
plane among the peaceful clover, but, climbing into the Hampden,
shut myself in war.

BOY:

I wish they'd let me go in to see my brother. They say he has
spasms of amnesia. I don't reckon he's normal now. That bloody
bomb blew up only inches from where he was standing....

MAN:

I thought you said he was shot?

BOY:

He was! And there was a bomb!

MAN:

London had it bad during the blitz....

BOY:

It was terrible.

MAN:

Bombs fell like rain....

BOY:

I'd like to get my hands on the bastards!

MAN:

No building was safe....

BOY:

I could do with a sandwich....

MAN:

Houses. Churches. Hospitals.

BOY:

There's that nurse....

MAN:

Nowhere was safe....

BOY:

I'll ask her if I can get one....

MAN:

I got a forty-eight hour pass. Couldn't spare me any longer. I was stationed in Dover. Artillery. Barbara was in London. In the thick of it....

BOY:

She says she'll bring me one....

MAN:

I had to come up in order to....

BOY:

And she reckons I'll have a long wait....

MAN:

Nowhere was safe....

BOY:

He's undergoing some type of therapy....

MAN:

London wasn't....

SISTER:

Their feet on London, their heads in the grey clouds, the Bank Holiday....

NURSE:

If you can call it a holiday!

SISTER:

The Bank Holiday crowds stroll from street to street cocking an eye for where the angel used to be in the sky. But the Happy Future is a thing of the past and the street echoes nothing but their dawdling feet.

NURSE:

The Lord's my shepherd.

SISTER:

Familiar words of myth stand up better to bombs than a granite monolith. Perhaps there is something in them?

NURSE:

I'll not want.

MAN:

Not when I'm dead.

NURSE:

He makes me down to lie.

MAN:

Death my christening and fire my font.

NURSE:

The quiet....

MAN:

Thames' or Dons' or Salweens'....

NURSE:

Waters by.

ALL:

Amen....

BOY:

It's funny....

MAN:

Amen....

BOY:

I get the strange feeling that I know you from somewhere?

MAN:

You've probably seen me in here....

BOY:

No! I told you - this is my first visit!

MAN:

Never a day passes....

BOY:

Can't remember where? But I know I've seen you before. Not that it matters....

NURSE:

Here you are, Rob.

BOY:

Thanks.

NURSE:

Everything alright, Mr. Wallace?

MAN:

I'm telling this young lad about....

BOY:

Ham sandwiches. I like ham. Will I be able to talk to the doctor about....?

NURSE:

There's nothing to worry about. He's the best. His methods have rarely been known to fail. You'll see.

MAN:

I've known him for a number of years. I have the greatest respect...

NURSE:

Dr. Morris believes in kindness and understanding. He's like a saint. And, now, duty calls....

BOY:

I thought she was going to sit with us. She smells so nice. Quite turns me on....

MAN:

The greatest respect....

BOY:

Were you always in Dover?

MAN:

No. I spent a lot of time in various places throughout the country....

BOY:

I thought you were shot up at Dunkirk? Surely that put you out of action?

MAN:

What?

BOY:

They're staring at us again....

MAN:

I didn't think I was that badly hurt. They said....

BOY:

I'm not interested in what they said! It's bad enough having to sit here listening to you without hearing about what they said!

MAN:

You don't have to stay with me....

BOY:

Where else is there to go?

MAN:

I thought you were pleased to talk with me?

BOY:

Oh Christ! Get on with your bloody story if it's going to keep you happy?

MAN:

I....

BOY:

I'm sorry. Really. You'll have to excuse me if I appear a bit on edge. What with this place and them two always staring....

MAN:

Thought you liked the nurse?

BOY:

Yes. But that bloody sister gives me the bloody creeps. She's weird.
The very look of her is enough to drive a bloke off his bleeding
rocker!

MAN:

They said....

BOY:

Get on with it!

MAN:

They said I'd spend the duration - well away from the front-line
battle....

BOY:

What's the time?

MAN:

Many of my mates were posted to every corner of the globe.
Europe. Africa. The far East. Had letters from a lot of them.
Kept me in touch with what was happening. Our Elsie had a chap
who was serving with Montgomery in the desert....

BOY:

I hate this bloody waiting!

MAN:

Martin, his name was....

BOY:

It's getting stuffy....

MAN:

I remember she made a scrap-book of all his letters and bits and
pieces from the papers.

BOY:

No air. Wouldn't care to be cooped up in this place every day and
night. I'd go spare....

MAN:

She met him a couple of weeks after war had been declared. Bit of a flirt, my sister. Had boyfriends in all the services! Probably could have started an army of her own!

BOY:

Close your eyes and think of England, eh?

MAN:

She wasn't like that!

BOY:

I believe you! I believe you!

MAN:

Nice sort of bloke was Martin. Officer. Not really in our class but nice all the same. No airs and graces. Came from Winchester. Elsie met him at a dance on Southampton Pier. Silly sod got himself killed at Arnheim....

BOY:

A Bridge Too Far....

MAN:

What?

BOY:

It's a film. I saw it on the telly....

MAN:

Films! Hollywood gloss!

BOY:

I think it was British?

MAN:

All the same - the glorification of war! Nothing about....

BOY:

The unsung heroes?

MAN:

Exactly!

BOY:

The men who fought for God know's what? The men who died in foreign places - men, who like you, like my brother, badly wounded, ending up in a place like this!

MAN:

I'm only visiting....

BOY:

I know that. What I mean is that you did....

MAN:

Yes.

BOY:

Winchester? Funny. Robin's regiment is based there. The Green Jackets. Did most of his training there. And in Wales. Brecon. Know it? You must do. Seems to me the whole sodding army does their basic training in Brecon....

MAN:

Did mine on Salisbury Plain....

BOY:

Beautiful place, though. Nice mountains....

MAN:

On Sal....?

BOY:

Brecon!

MAN:

You been there?

BOY:

No! I - I got a postcard from Robin!

MAN:

I see....

BOY:

His first posting was to Belfast. Should never be allowed. Let them sort out their own differences....

MAN:

Got to go where they send you....

BOY:

But bloody Northern Ireland? It's like sending lambs to the slaughter. Mere kids. Take my brother. He's seventeen. Seventeen! Want me to spell it out to you? No experience of the joys of youth hood. And now he's been blown up by some terrorist's booby-trap....

MAN:

Happens all the time....

BOY:

What a waste! What a bloody waste!

MAN:

Take it easy. What's done is done....

BOY:

It's okay for you. You've had your life. What is there for him? This place? My God! What kind of life is that?

MAN:

Don't take on so. Here. Have a sweet. I always have some with me. Take one....

BOY:

Stuff them!

MAN:

Adventure, among other things, attracts the young men to the Forces nowadays. They've got a choice. We hadn't....

BOY:

Choice! Between what and the dole queue? It's all very well. Join the Professionals for a better life! Smart uniform....

MAN:

Attracts the girls....

BOY:

Perhaps?

MAN:

That's all they think about when they join up! No thought about fighting and the likelihood of getting killed. Oh no! That only happens in books. Never in the real world....

SISTER:

Living in a wide landscape are the flowers. Rosenburg I only repeat what you are saying. The shell and the hawk, every hour, are slaying men and jerboas, slaying the mind. But the body can fill the hungry flowers. And the dogs who cry words at night are the most hostile things of all. But that is not new. Each time the night discards draperies on the eyes and leaves the mind awake I look each side of the door of sleep for the little coin it will take to buy the secret I shall not keep.

MAN:

Lay the coin on my tongue and I will sing of what others have never set eyes on.

DOCTOR:

The red rock wilderness shall be my dwelling-place. Where the wind saws at the bluffs and the pebble falls like thunder I shall watch the clawed sun tear the rocks assunder. The seven-branched cactus will never sweat wine. My own bleeding feet shall furnish the sign. The rock says....

SISTER:

Endure.

DOCTOR:

The wind says....

SISTER:

Pursue.

DOCTOR:

The sun says....

MAN:

I will suck your bones and afterwards bury you.

BOY:

You might be right about what you said....

                              MAN:

What?

                              BOY:

The uniforms. The birds do tend to flock around the squaddies and
the like.! Fellers like me don't stand a chance....

                              MAN:

Like you?

                              BOY:

Yes! I'm bloody unlikely to....

                              MAN:

What?

                              BOY:

Oh nothing. Nothing! Anyhow - what would you care?

                             SISTER:

Everything alright here?

                              MAN:

We're just talking....

                             SISTER:

That's good.

                              BOY:

You lot believe in keeping us waiting, don't you? Bloody National
Health! Bet you wouldn't let someone in here who's dying! They'd
have to wait until a bloody bed was available! Here we are, us
two, come into visit. Been waiting what seems like hours. We're
becoming a part of the furniture!

                             SISTER:

I'm afraid you'll have to be patient....

                              BOY:

And all you can do is stare at us. What's the matter with us? We
are human, aren't we? Just like any other bugger!

                             SISTER:

Well! I'll have to get the doctor....

BOY:

You do that!

SISTER:

He'll be very upset if I repeat what you've been saying.

BOY:

Sweet on him, are you? Bet you can find a spare bed for you-know-what when the need arises!

SISTER:

Really!

BOY:

Any chance for me with that nurse? Got a free bed for....?

MAN:

What work do you do?

BOY:

Eh?

MAN:

Work?

BOY:

Oh....

MAN:

Get good pay nowadays. Not like when I was a lad. Got very little. I was an apprentice when I left school....

BOY:

So you said. For a builder.

MAN:

Seven and six is all I got....thirty-seven and a half pence!

BOY:

Bit of a bitch that sister....

MAN:

Better now. Good money. With money in your pocket you can ave the women falling at you feet....

BOY:

That doctor's welcome to her....

MAN:

That's all they want nowadays. New this. New that. And the man has to pay. Equality? Who says anything about equality? Still. Plenty of money about. I bet the youth of today of today aren't short of a bob or two? That's what it was all about, you know - the war. A better future for our kids....

BOY:

Some bloody rotten future! Fighting in most places of the world. Threat of a nuclear holocaust if anyone panics and presses the button. And the likes of me? The youth you reckon are so bloody loaded with the ready? Come off it! You talk as if you've been shut away for years. Completely out of touch with the world as it is now....

MAN:

Pardon?

BOY:

Some life! Every other week down the Labour to sign on. Great future! Be better off six feet under and pushing up the bleeding daisies!

MAN:

You should follow your brother's example. Join up.

BOY:

What?

MAN:

Join up. You watch the telly. Haven't you seen the adverts. It's a man's world in the....

BOY:

Sod the Professionals!

MAN:

This would be a worse place if it wasn't for the fighting men. We fought for you!

BOY:

Piss off!

MAN:

Join up. Quit the streets. Don't suffer the dole queue for the rest of your life!

NURSE:

Yes. We are going to suffer now.

SISTER:

The sky throbs like a feverish forehead.

NURSE:

Pain is real.

SISTER:

The groping searchlights suddenly reveal the little natures that will make us cry, who never quite believed they could exist, not where we were.

NURSE:

They take us by surprise like ugly long-forgotten memories, and, like a conscience, the guns resist.

SISTER:

Behind such sociable home-loving eye the private massacres are taking place. All women, Jews, the Rich, the Human Race.

NURSE:

The mountains cannot judge us when we lie.

SISTER:

We dwell upon the earth.

NURSE:

The earth obeys the intelligent and evil till they die.

BOY:

Be better off dead....

MAN:

You shouldn't say that....

BOY:

I'm sorry. I really don't know what came over me. Tell me some more about the war. It'll help to take my mind off things.

MAN:

Right.

BOY:

I promise I'll listen....

MAN:

Jerry wasn't content with sending the Luftwaffe over to bomb us. He had to do more. Flying bombs. The V2. Doodlebugs. I was stationed in London then. Not the best of places to be. But, at least, I was near Barbara. That made all the difference. Suppose I was as good as out of the war. In a manner of speaking, that is. Things were pretty quiet on the home front....

BOY:

What about the bombs?

MAN:

It wasn't so bad. We used to shelter in the underground. Community spirit. We used to have a laugh....

BOY:

A laugh?

MAN:

Had to keep cheerful....

BOY:

With all them doodlebugs?

MAN:

And we had the assurances that the war was nearly at an end. Churchill and the other top brass were busy organising the Normandy Invasion....

BOY:

I've been there.

MAN:

Where?

BOY:

Stupid old sod! Where do you think? The bloody moon? Normandy! You've just mentioned the place. I went on a day trip with my aunt when I was on holiday in St. Helier. I told you about my uncle. Aunt Dominique was his widow. We went to St. Malo. Her family were from there originally.

MAN:
I think that's in Brittany?

BOY:
Normandy or Brittany. What's the difference? They're both in bloody France, aren't they?

MAN:
Yes.

BOY:
Well, then! Did you take part in D-Day?

MAN:
wound was playing up quite a bit and I was always in and out of hospital. Even to this day I can't really say I've completely recovered.

BOY:
Eh?

MAN:
Nothing.

BOY:
Um. You're not a patient in this place, are you? A part of the hospital is where they keep the nutters. You're not one, are you? Well?

MAN:
I did try to. I volunteered....

BOY:
Are you?

MAN:
I wanted a chance to get back at Jerry for what he'd done to me and....

BOY:
Guess you're right about joining up....

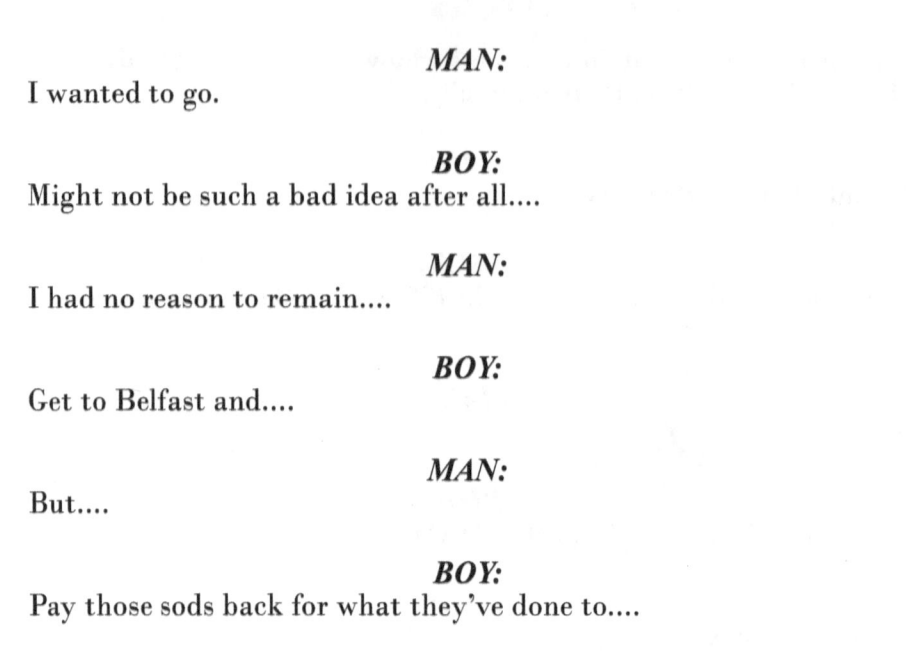

MAN:

I wanted to go.

BOY:

Might not be such a bad idea after all....

MAN:

I had no reason to remain....

BOY:

Get to Belfast and....

MAN:

But....

BOY:

Pay those sods back for what they've done to....

DOCTOR:

One evening, breaking a jeep journey at Capuzzo, I noticed a soldier as he entered the cemetery and stood looking at the grave of a fallen enemy.

BOY:

Here's another good Jerry. Poor mucker. Just seventeen. Must be hard up for manpower. Or else he volunteered, silly bastard. That's the fatal, the fatal mistake. Never volunteer for nothing. I wonder how he died? Just as well it was him and not one of our chaps. Yes. Yes. The only good Jerry, as they say,
is your sort, chum. Cheerio, you poor bastard. Don't be late on parade when the Lord calls "Close Order". Keep waiting for the angels. Keep listening for reveille....

DOCTOR:

Everything alright?

SISTER:

I must strongly complain as to the attitude of that boy....

NURSE:

He's very pleasant....

SISTER:

To you, maybe. But he has been extremely rude to me....

DOCTOR:

Then you will have to excuse his manner. He is going through a very traumatic experience.

SISTER:

Yes, doctor....

BOY:

They're at it again....

MAN:

What?

BOY:

Staring....

MAN:

Ignore them....

BOY:

Worse than being in prison!

MAN:

Arnold was....

BOY:

Who?

MAN:

Arnold.

BOY:

Oh. Your brother-in-law.

MAN:

He was a prisoner-of-war.

BOY:

So you said.

MAN:

He reckoned they didn't have it too bad. The Jerry guards some of them - were alright. So Arnold reckoned....

DOCTOR:

Keep alert. We must be on our guard, We can't allow a sudden
relapse. If that occurred things might well turn into an extremely
dangerous situation. Such patients find uncontrollable strength.
We'd never be able to contain him. He'd run. And escape would be
most serious....

MAN:

He got quite friendly with some of the guards, They were human
just like us. They had families and loved ones. No difference really.
Just happened to be on the other side....

BOY:

Those bastards in the IRA! Loved ones! Bloody scum....

MAN:

He palled up with one in particular. They both had similar
imterests. Both were students before the war. Both studied
literature. Neither particularly wanted to fight. So....

BOY:

Murderers....

MAN:

After the war they kept in contact. Used to visit each other.
Arnold often went to Munich for a holiday and Kurt, the German
chap, came over here a few times. Nice enough bloke. Rather quiet.
I met him once or twice. He visited me....

BOY:

What I wouldn't do to them!

MAN:

Lived near Dachau. You heard of the place? Must have done! One
of those bloody concentration camps was near there. Those poor
sods never stood a chance. Of course we didn't know too much
about them. Not till the war was over. Even Kurt told me that
people living near the camps didn't really know what
was going on in them....

BOY:

I've seen pictures of the Jews....

MAN:

Makes you wonder how anybody could treat another human being in such a way? Locked up. Starved. Used for those horrendous experiments. Butchered. And burnt....

BOY:

Those bastards in Ireland ought to get that kind of treatment. Round them all up and gas the lot....

MAN:

We knew nothing of that horror....

BOY:

Christ! How can anybody have treated those poor bastards like that?

NURSE:

Remember the blackness of that flesh tarring the bones with a thin varnish.

DOCTOR:

Belsen.

SISTER:

Theresenstadt.

MAN:

Buchenwald.

BOY:

Where faces were a clenched despair knocking at the bird-song fretted air.

NURSE:

Their eyes sunk jellied in their holes were held up to the sun like begging bowls, their hands like rakes with finger-nails of rust scratched for a little kindness from the dust. To many, in it's beak, no dove brought answer.

DOCTOR:

Never a day passes but I remember them, their stone-blind faces beated by arclights, their eyes turned inward seeking an answer and their passage homeward, dreaming of the Promised Land and next year in Jerusalem.

NURSE:

But, being citizens of time, they would never learn the body's nationality. Tortured for years now, they refuse to sever spirit from flesh or accept our callow century.

DOCTOR:

Not without hope, but lacking present solace, the preacher knows the feel of nails and grace.

NURSE:

The singer snores. The orator's facile hands are fixed in a gesture no-one understands. Others escaped, yet paid for their betrayal. Even the politicians with their stale visions and cheap flirtations with the past will not die any easier at the last.

DOCTOR:

The ones who took to garrets and consumption in foreign cities, found a dungeon deeper than any Dachau. Free but still confined the human lack of pity split their mind. Whatever days, whatever seasons pass, the prisoners must stare in pain's face, until, at last, the courage they have learned shall burst the walls and overturn the world.

BOTH:

We will remember them.

ALL:

We will remember.

BOY:

Wonder if I can see our kid yet? Must be awful shut up the way he is....

MAN:

The nurse will let you know....

BOY:

Where is she? Nurse! Where's she bloody gone?

MAN:

She's probably busy. Making plans for....

BOY:

Reckon those bastards mean to carry out more bombings?

MAN:

That's what I heard. So, you see, the staff will be making preparations in order to cope with an emergency. They have to come up with necessary solutions before the bloody problems arise.

DOCTOR:

I charge you to take any steps necessary towards a general solution to the Jewish problem in the areas of German influence in Europe.

SISTER:

The final solution will be applied to about eleven million people....

DOCTOR:

Not people! Vermin!

SISTER:

The Jews will be transferred to the east under close surveillance and there assigned to force labour.

BOY:

Many of them will be naturally eliminated by physical deficiency.

SISTER:

Those who survive will be dealt with accordingly.

DOCTOR:

Good. The Jewish filth will no longer present a threat to our glorious Reich.

MAN:

The extermination programme. That's what they called it....

BOY:

Did your brother-in-law ever get to see any of those camps?

MAN:

What?

BOY:

The ones where they burned the Jews?

MAN:

Only after the war. Terrible sight, he said. Was going to write a book about it all. Never did, though....

BOY:

He was a writer, then?

MAN:

No. Worked as a reporter for the BBC. Did do a programme about the liberation of Belsen. He was there....

BOY:

In Belsen? Thought that was only for the Jews?

MAN:

Arnold was among the liberators....

BOY:

Oh....

MAN:

He was set free a week or so before the end of hostilities and, like everybody else, helped wherever he could....

BOY:

I see....

MAN:

Must be time for visiting?

BOY:

Didn't I say that a few minutes ago?

MAN:

Barbara will be worried....

BOY:

She won't be the only one. It's funny....

MAN:

What is?

BOY:

Just a feeling....

MAN:

What kind of feeling?

BOY:

Of becoming a part of the furniture. I seem to know every square inch of these bloody walls. I've been sitting here listening to you and staring at blank walls! I reckon I know every stain, every brush mark. A bloody fly has been buzzing around and shitting all over the place. All the time. Buzzing here.
Buzzing there. Trying to find a way out. I bet it's impossible to escape....?

MAN:

It's safe in here.

BOY:

There it is!

MAN:

Where?

BOY:

Over there! I'm going to take a swipe at it!

MAN:

Don't!

BOY:

You bastard! That's better. I got the sod. Dead. Bloody vermin!

MAN:

What did you do that for? It wasn't doing any harm. One of God's creatures. Just like you and me....

BOY:

I hate the things. Indoors especially. Alright outside where they belong. But not in here. Not in a hospital. You'd think they'd take a bit of care? Germ-ridden buggers....

DOCTOR:

There are five apple trees here, standing in a row. One day, when the wind began to blow, I watched the petals falling into the ditch below. Beyond the wire is an orchard full of apple thickly strewn over the grass below. In my garden in England, an apple tree stands. Today the petals are fluttering over
her hands while she is gathering the bluebells and the celandines below.

BOY:

Bet my brother will be pleased to see me. He looks up to me. The eldest and all that....

MAN:

You're on the dole. That's not much to look up to!

BOY:

So what?

MAN:

How old are you?

BOY:

What do you want to know for?

MAN:

No reason.

BOY:

If you must know I'm a year older than my brother.

MAN:

Oh. My Barbara - she'll be glad to see me....

BOY:

Of course she will. I bet she's in there now, eh, combing her hair, keeping her eyes on the clock and the door....

MAN:

She knows I never miss a day. I never miss....

BOY:

I'll be in here every day to see our kid now that they've moved him nearer home.

MAN:

Even though you don't like the smell of this place?

BOY:

Get used to it. Have to for his sake. I'm all he's got really. My parents were killed a few years ago in a car crash. I did have a brother - another one, that is.

MAN:

It was a living hell with those Jerries dropping bombs all around us....

BOY:

Action stations!

DOCTOR:

Tin hats and apprehension!

SISTER:

Rush to guns and hoses. Engine room and wireless office.

NURSE:

Air of tension.

BOY:

Eyes uplifted and some seawards gazing.

DOCTOR:

Ears are straining for a distant....

ALL:

Boom!

SISTER:

Roar of engines.

NURSE:

Lips are phrasing prayers, maybe, or cursing the Hun.

BOY:

Friendly aircraft in the distant loom and are gone.

DOCTOR:

Minutes pass.

MAN:

Carry on!

ALL:

Carry on!

BOY:

I live with my gran now. I was only ten when we buried them....

MAN:

I awake some nights and I imagine I hear the screaming of those V2s.

BOY:

My brother wakes screaming. So they say. Must be worse for him now. In this place. All shut in. Nothing but white walls. White uniforms. Flies. Roses by the bedside.

MAN:

Blood-red roses....

BOY:

Blood-red.

MAN:

By her bedside....

BOY:

I hate blood....

MAN:

Pink roses on the wallpaper dripping blood....

BOY:

Face. Arms. Legs. All covered....

MAN:

It was a nice little flat....

BOY:

I hate blood.

NURSE:

With grey arm twisted over a green face the dust of passing trucks swirls over him, lying by the roadside in his proper place, for he had crossed the ultimate far rim that hides us from the valley of the dead. He lies like used equipment thrown aside, of which our swift advance can take no heed, roses, triumphal cars.

SISTER:

But this one died.

NURSE:

Once war memorials, pitiful attempt in some vague way regretfully to atone for those lost futures that the dead had dreamt, covered the land with their lamenting stone.

SISTER:

But in our hearts we bear a heavier load. The bodies of the dead beside the road.

NURSE:

They carry no shadow in sunlight, the past like a slate rubbed out in the future that arrived too late.

SISTER:

Their faces are maps of a landscape, where ghosts hover around them, an arena of ruins that are all alike each other.

NURSE:

And their words are a babel whose meaning is plain. The shadow of Cain has been thrown onto Abel. So, unseen, the derelict cities crowd in on their eyes.

SISTER:

But self-pity has grown and conditioned surprise.

BOY:

Now nothing is important, enormous or true.

DOCTOR:

The message was too long delayed. They are part of their passage.

NURSE:

The long shadow has turned into stone.

SISTER:

The pillar salt not a wife.

MAN:

And death, too, is over - like life....

BOY:

Did I hear the bell? Did you hear it?

MAN:

They ring it at the end of visiting....

BOY:

Oh yes. I remember you mentioning it....

MAN:

Any sign of other visitors?

BOY:

Not yet....

MAN:

Not yet....

BOY:

So. You come here every day. Christ! You must be some kind of martyr? She really must be something, this missus of yours?

MAN:

She is at that....

BOY:

How were things at the end of the war? I bet you and....

MAN:

Barbara.

BOY:

Yeah. I bet you and her hit a few high spots on VE night, eh?

MAN:

What?

BOY:

VE night! You must have celebrated? Well? Did you?

MAN:

Questions! Questions! Don't you ever get fed up with asking so many questions?

BOY:

I thought you....?

MAN:

Look. I've enjoyed your company. I really have. But don't ask me any more questions! That's all I ever get! Questions! Questions! Always questions in this place....

BOY:

Sorry! I don't mean to upset you. Was it something I said?

MAN:

There you are, you see. More questions!

BOY:

I said I'm sorry. What else can I say? I've only come here to visit my brother. You spoke to me first. Don't forget that! I never wanted to get into conversation with you. An old man! A lonely old man! That's all you are! I only chatted because I felt sorry for you. I could have done more with my time than wasting it talking to you. I could have chatted up that nurse.

MAN:

Is that all you think about? I've only ever had one woman in all my life....

BOY:

So? What am I expected to do about that? Recommend you for a bleeding medal?

MAN:

Nurse!

BOY:

A lonely old man!

MAN:

Nurse!

BOY:

What's the point of calling her? She won't help. All the same in here. Too busy to worry about the likes of us!

MAN:

Nurse!

NURSE:

What's the matter, Mr. Wallace?

MAN:

This young bugger....

BOY:

I think I upset him. I said I was sorry.

NURSE:

Don't worry....

BOY:

I said I was sorry....

NURSE:

I'm sure you did.

MAN:

I don't like too many questions....

NURSE:

We thought you were enjoying talking to....

BOY:

He was....

NURSE:

There you are then....

MAN:

I'm sorry....

NURSE:

You'll soon be seeing....

MAN:

My Barbara? I want to be with her....

NURSE:

Yes, dear, yes....

MAN:

Good.

NURSE:

Perhaps I could bring you a cup of tea?

MAN:

No thank you. I'm alright. Getting a bit over excited, that's all. A bit dizzy. And my eyes seem to be getting rather tired.

BOY:

Look, Mike, I'm really sorry - honest I am. Forgive me....

MAN:

Forget it. I'm just a silly old man who should....

NURSE:

That's better....

BOY:

I feel bloody miserable now. No reason to go upsetting an old bloke like you. I admire you. You've done so much. I only hope I'm like you when I'm old....

MAN:

Don't hope that....

BOY:

Why?

MAN:

Just don't! Anyhow. Let's forget everything. Cheer up. Look on the bright side. Your brother'll be glad to see you. Just like my Florence Nightingale will be pleased when I'm by her side. Two of a kind, you and I. Cheer up....

SISTER:

Thunder gathers all the sky.

MAN:

Tomorrow night a war will end.

NURSE:

Men their natural deaths may die and Cain shall be his brother's friend.

SISTER:

From the lethal clouds of lead thickening hatred shall descend in fruitful rain upon the head.

BOY:

Tomorrow night a war will end.

NURSE:

Thunder mock not Abel's cry.

DOCTOR:

Let this symbolic storm expend the sum of man's malignity.

NURSE:

And Cain shall be his brother's friend.

SISTER:

There are no words to be said.

DOCTOR:

Let the future recommend the living to the luckless dead.

MAN/BOY:

Tomorrow night a war will end.

BOY:

You're right, of course. No need to get worked up about nothing. I'm really sorry.

MAN:

Don't worry about it. It's this place. Bound to make you a bit anxious. A bit depressed....

BOY:

Down the corridor and turn right. I think I'll make my way along to the ward. Our kid'll be over the moon to see me. Hope your wife is okay. All the best. It was nice talking to you. Really. Probably see you again sometime....

MAN:

Yes. See you again. I'm always in here. Part of the furniture, you could say....

BOY:
I must know every square inch of these bleeding walls....

MAN:
See you. Not a bad sort of nipper - for the younger generation, that is.

BOY:(off)
No! No! No!

MAN:
Looks like it's going to be busy tonight.

BOY:(off)
No more bombs!

MAN:
Yes. There goes the sirens. Hope Barbara will be alright in that hospital. Those Jerries don't care where they drop there bloody bombs. More innocent sods'll meet their Maker tonight – that's for sure. Nice wallpaper. I honestly do like roses....

DOCTOR:
It is false that I wanted or anyone in Germany wanted war.
The war was sought and provoked exclusively by international politicians belonging to the Jewish race or working for the Jews. The numerous offers that I made to disarm are there to testify before posterity that responsibility cannot be ascribed to me. I said, often enough, after the First World War, that I had no desire at all to fight Great Britain. Nor did I want war with the United States. In times to come the ruins of our cities will
keep alive hatred for those who bear the real responsibility for our martyrdom. The agents of international Jewry. National Socialism is dead. We have lost the game. All that remains is for us to die worthily.

NURSE:
So declared Hitler in his Will dated the twenty-ninth of April nineteen-forty-five.

SISTER:
The following afternoon Adolf Hitler and his mistress, Eva Braun, took their lives in the Berlin bunker. Eight days later the war was over in Europe....

DOCTOR:

It is finished. The enormous dust-cloud over Europe lifts like a million swallows. And a light, drifting in craters, touches the quiet dead.

NURSE:

Now, at the bugle's hour, before the blood cakes in a clean wind hung like a medal on the smoky noon whitens the bones that feeds the earth, before the wheat-ear springs green again in the green spring.

SISTER:

And they are bread in the bodies of the young, be strong to remember how the bread died, screaming....

DOCTOR:

Gangrene was corn.

NURSE

And monuments went mad.

ALL:

We will remember.

NURSE:

Thank God for peace in our time.

MAN:

Barbara! Barbara? Oh! I remember now! Oh Barbara....

NURSE:

What is it, Mr. Wallace?

MAN:

I remember! I remember!

NURSE:

I'll get the doctor....

MAN:

Why did they have to get you? Oh Barbara. You never did anyone any wrong. You only thought of the good of others. Those bastards didn't give a damn! A direct hit! Men, women, children. What chance did they have? Innocent people. The hospital. Nothing but rubble. I tore at the bricks. Days and

days I dug. I couldn't find you. I couldn't find you. I knew you
were dead but still I searched. What was the point? It just didn't
matter. It didn't matter. He's a nice lad. You would like him,
Barbara. We should have had a son. But you died and the baby
you were carrying....

BOY:

I couldn't find him. I looked but he wasn't there. I went straight
down the corridor and turned right. Just as you said. Just as the
nurse said. But I couldn't find him. It was so dark. Then. Then I
saw the flash! Then the explosion! My God! Bodies. Blood. Only
minutes before we were laughing and joking.
The officer shouted some orders! Voices echoed through the
carnage. Voices of my friends. Then. Then nothing....

MAN:

Nothing matters anymore.

BOY:

Nothing....

MAN:

One bomb, one mighty bomb....

BOY:

White walls. White uniforms. Figures, unseen faces, standing over
me. Blood-red roses....

MAN:

One bomb....

BOY:

One bomb. One mighty bomb. Too many people have died. Too
many people will die. For what? My parents? Why did they have
to die? And him? Robert. Only nine years old. He was going to be
a General! Patton was his hero. Poor, poor boy. Such a waste. Oh
God! Don't let me go back to that hell of a place....!

MAN:

Nothing matters anymore....

BOY:

Nothing....

MAN:

Barbara....

BOY:

Nurse! Nurse! Nurse! Where the bloody hell is she? Nurse!

MAN:

You're wasting your time. They're always too busy in here to bother with the likes of us....

BOY:

Put a bloody sock in it! Nurse! Oh. Mike. I'm sorry. Speak to me. Mike? Mike! Nurse! Nurse! Nurse!

NURSE:

Yes, Robin? What is it?

BOY:

I think he's dead....

NURSE:

Come along now. Everything will be alright. He's with her now. Hold on to me.

BOY:

Today was a beautiful day. The sky was a brilliant blue.

DOCTOR:

And we laugh it off.

SISTER:

And go round town in the evening....

NURSE:

Come. This way. There's a good boy. Down the corridor and turn right....

CURTAIN

Biography

Michael Nash, originally from Hampshire, has written several works for the stage including "Public Heroes Private Friends," and "Signs of Fire," a musical about the last year in the life of Van Gogh. Nash has been employed as a writer, a teacher of Drama and English, a publisher, and all around artist. His interests include cooking, computing, and travel, especially to Turkey and Istanbul, where Nash received a degree from Istanbul University. Involved in over twenty stage productions, onstage and off, Nash has been an active participant appearing in both amateur and professional productions including "Under Milkwood," "A Man for All Seasons," and "The Pajama Game." "They're Dropping Bombs Not Ham Sandwiches" takes place in a hospital corridor and is a dialogue between a WWII veteran and a young man embroiled in the troubles of Northern Ireland. This is Nash's tenth completed work for the stage. Michael Nash currently resides in Middlesbrough.

www.ingramcontent.com/pod-product-compliance
Lightning Source LLC
Chambersburg PA
CBHW021426200626
46814CB00015B/1600